Blast off!

"Leave me alone," Ben bellowed again. "I'm staying."

"Ben, you're making a mistake," Cassie panted as she and Zeke began to drag the bully across the floor of the spaceship.

But it was too late. The engines roared, the ship lurched, and suddenly Cassie felt as if the world had dropped from under her. She, Zeke, and Ben all raced for the window—and watched the Earth grow small beneath them.

Look for the next exciting book in the series
The Spy from Outer Space

Spies, Incorporated

Available now!

ESCAPE FROM EARTH

Debra Hess

Illustrated by Carol Newsom

Hyperion Paperbacks for Children
New York

Produced by Chardiet Unlimited, Inc., 33 West 17th Street,
New York, New York 10011.
A Hyperion Paperback original
First edition: May 1994

1   3   5   7   9   10   8   6   4   2

Library of Congress Cataloging-in-Publication Data

Hess, Debra
Escape from Earth/Debra Hess; illustrated by Carol Newsom—1st ed.
    p.   cm.—(The spy from outer space; #3)
Summary: Cassie and her friend Zeke, a boy from outer space, try to
uncover the meaning behind a mysterious message left on board his
ship, while dealing with the suspicions of Ben, the class bully.
ISBN 1-56282-682-4
[1. Extraterrestrial beings—Fiction. 2. Science Fiction. 3. Mystery and
detective stories.]
I. Newsom, Carol, ill.   II. Title.   III. Series: Hess, Debra. Spy from
outer space; #3.
PZ7.H4326Es   1994
[Fic]—dc20   93-35494
CIP
AC

FOR SUSANNE K.—temporarily grounded on Earth

ESCAPE FROM EARTH

The envelope lay on the table unopened, the words Top Secret beckoning to Cassie. She had to sit on her hands to keep from grabbing the package and ripping open the seal.

"Hey, Spot," she called into the next room of the spaceship. "Did Zeke tell you when he'd be back?"

When there was no response to her question, Cassie got up and peered into the adjoining room. Spot was nowhere to be seen. Cassie grinned and flew back to the table. Grabbing the oversize envelope, she moved toward the center of the room, where a large cylinder of bubbling, spitting liquid gave off a powerful glow. Then Cassie Williams, fifth-grade Super Sleuth, reached into her spy belt and removed a high-powered magnifying glass. She held the envelope up to the light, and she tried to read the contents.

"Cease this action immediately, or I will have

to ask you to remove yourself from the ship," a voice commanded from behind her.

Cassie jumped and dropped the envelope. Then, laughing at herself, she picked it up and turned to face her accuser.

"Sorry, Spot," she said, grinning sheepishly at the small robot who stood before her. "I'll just put this on the table." She slid the envelope back to where it belonged.

"It will be necessary to report your behavior to Zeke," Spot's mechanical voice droned at Cassie.

"No, it won't," said Cassie. She stared at the robot, trying to figure out what was different about him. Suddenly it hit her.

"Hey—where are your dog wigs?"

Ever since they'd been accidentally stranded on Earth, all of the Triminicans had had to disguise themselves as Earth creatures. Spot hated the dog costume Zeke and Cassie had created for him, but he accepted that it was necessary if the aliens' presence was to remain a secret.

"I prefer not to wear the wigs when there is no chance of contact with Earthlings," stated Spot.

"Oh yeah?" said Cassie playfully. "What am I?"

"You do not count!" said Spot.

Just then a flashing light on the ship's control panel caught Cassie's eye.

"Spot, what's that?"

"That is merely the invisibility shield being momentarily deactivated by remote control."

3

"Zeke!" cried Cassie. She raced to the control panel and lowered the staircase for her alien friend. A moment later Zeke clambered on board. His eyes lit up when he saw Cassie.

"Am I late?" he asked.

"Yes," said Cassie, trying not to blurt out about the envelope right away. "But somehow I'm not surprised. How's Marilee?"

Zeke shrugged. Marilee Tischler, the most stuck-up girl in the fifth grade and Cassie's least favorite person on the face of the Earth, was Zeke's partner for the upcoming school science fair.

"She is pleasant enough. But she does not seem to have an aptitude for science. I did most of the work on our project myself."

"Well, what do you expect?" said Cassie, laughing. "I mean, a molecule-splitting experiment? Really, Zeke. Why don't you wear a sign on your shirt that says, 'Hi, I'm from another planet, and I'm smarter than you!'"

"It is a simple experiment that any eight year old can do on Triminica," said Zeke.

"Does that mean you finished it?" asked Cassie.

"Of course," said Zeke. "It *is* a required assignment. And it *is* due on Monday. By the way, how is the solar system?"

Cassie groaned. Marilee Tischler might not be a genius. But next to Cassie's partner, Ben O'Brien, she looked like one.

"It exploded," Cassie explained.

"You are not serious?" said Zeke, astounded.

"Unfortunately, I am."

"The whole solar system?"

"No, not exactly," said Cassie. "Just the sun, Earth, Mercury, and Venus."

"Oh, I see," said Zeke. "Ben insisted on wiring the sun to make it shine."

"It was a disaster," said Cassie. "We're going to have to spend the entire day tomorrow rebuilding those four planets."

"Why did you let him do it?" asked Zeke.

"Come on, Zeke," said Cassie. "Just because you used karate to beat him in one little fight, and just because we were able to trick him into helping us with our last spying problem, doesn't make Ben anything other than what he is: the class bully."

"He bullied you into letting him wire the sun?" asked Zeke.

Cassie nodded silently.

Zeke was thoughtful. "Perhaps I will withhold karate lessons from him if he continues to behave this way," he said finally.

Cassie opened her mouth to answer, but just then her eyes fell on the envelope on the table.

"Zeke!" she said, her eyes sparkling. "There's an envelope here that says Top Secret on it."

"Really?" said Zeke. "Who is it from?"

5

"I don't know," said Cassie.

"Well, how did it get here?" asked Zeke, peering at the mysterious package but not touching it.

"It seems to have appeared on the ship shortly after you departed," Spot reported.

"What do you mean 'appeared'?" asked Zeke.

"It was not there, and then it was," said Spot simply.

"Come on, Zeke. Open it," Cassie urged.

Zeke squinted at the bold black letters.

"We should dust it for fingerprints first," he announced.

"I told you not to touch it!" Spot said to Cassie.

"Cassie—you did not!" said Zeke.

Cassie smiled, embarrassed. "Sorry, Zeke. I was so curious, I guess I wasn't thinking."

"Cassie attempted to open the envelope without permission," Spot reported.

"I did not!" said Cassie.

"Yes, you did," said Spot.

"NO, I DIDN'T!" Cassie shouted.

"Yes, you did," Spot repeated calmly.

This was going to be worse than arguing with her five-year-old brother. Cassie smiled at Zeke and shrugged.

"Okay, okay. I tried to read the inside by holding it up to the light. But"—she glared at Spot—"I did *not* try to open it."

"That is all right," said Zeke. "I realize you

lack the training of the Interstellar Spy Academy."

Cassie groaned. It was true that on his planet Zeke attended a training school for real spies. Compared to him, Cassie was just a kid with a toy spy kit. But ever since Zeke and his family landed on Earth, Cassie and Zeke had been spying partners. And they would remain partners and best friends for as long as Zeke remained.

It was hard to tell how long that might be, though. Zeke's parents, Mirac and Inora, had gone to Hawaii to get the ingredients needed for the spaceship's fuel. Sometimes Cassie found herself hoping they would never return.

Zeke left the room for a moment and came back with a fingerprinting kit. Together he and Cassie dusted the envelope with the special powder. But the only prints they were able to lift were hers.

At last Zeke opened the envelope. Cassie held her breath while he slid out a single sheet of unfolded stationery. The paper was creamy in color, with a letterhead embossed in gold. It read:

T . O . E .

and that was it. There was no address, no name, no phone number. Just the three letters spread

out across the top of the page. Beneath them
someone had typed a message:

The house at the end of Whisper Wind Lane.

Knock twice, count four,
knock thrice, count six,
knock twice.

Midnight.
Or else.

We know who you are.

CHAPTER

2

"Or else . . . or else." The words echoed over and over in Cassie's mind as she strolled toward the house at the end of Whisper Wind Lane. With her hands shoved into her jacket pockets and her feet kicking casually at the pebbles and leaves in her path, she looked just like any other ten-year-old girl out for a walk. Except, of course, for two very important facts.

1. As far as she knew, there wasn't a ten year old on Earth whose parents would allow her to be out walking alone at eleven thirty at night—even if it *was* Saturday night; and

2. *No one ever went* alone *to the house at the end of Whisper Wind Lane.*

After all, the old mansion had been abandoned for as long as anyone in Hillsdale could remember. And it had been haunted for at least as long as Cassie had been alive. How had she let Zeke and Spot talk her into this, anyway?

It was all Spot's fault, Cassie thought as she bravely continued walking. Zeke had wanted to go himself. But as soon as the robot saw the "or else" part of the note, he had started spewing forth the "I am programmed to protect Zeke" speech that Cassie had heard so often. It was true that Mirac and Inora had left Spot behind to protect Zeke. It was also true that if Zeke's identity was discovered, the Triminicans might never be allowed to return to their planet. But at this particular moment, alone, walking toward the scariest place in Hillsdale, Cassie really wished that Zeke was with her. "Or else, or else, or else . . ."

Cassie took a deep breath and focused her eyes on the rickety old house. It loomed in front of her, layer upon layer of cobwebs glistening in the light of the moon. Cassie shivered and then reminded herself that spies are brave. But the closer she got, the harder it was to stop her legs from shaking.

Finally she reached the front yard. Crouching in the shadow of a large weeping willow tree, Cassie pulled out a walkie-talkie from her pocket. It was one of two that came with her Super Deluxe Spy Kit. As a kind of reward to Cassie for going to the house, Spot had used his technical skills to soup up the communications device. It now had a range of twenty miles!

Cassie held the walkie-talkie in one hand and

kept the other hand in her pocket, curled around her ray gun—just in case. It wasn't a real ray gun. Zeke wouldn't be issued one of those until he graduated from the spy academy. But the toy version that he had lent Cassie had other important features that a spy might need, one of which was a switch on the side that activated a high-powered screech. It was loud enough to scare anyone away. Except maybe a ghost.

"I'm in position," Cassie said into her walkie-talkie.

The walkie-talkie crackled back at her. A second later Zeke's voice came through loud and clear.

"Report!"

"Old abandoned house," said Cassie. "It looks just as spooky as it ever has, except for maybe the time on Halloween when Melinda and I—"

Zeke interrupted her. "Cassie, stick to the situation at hand," he crackled in her ear.

"Fine," snapped Cassie. "As long as you stop using my real name."

There was silence on the other end. And then . . .

"Good point, agent Earthling. Continue your report."

Cassie giggled nervously. Then she unzipped her jacket and removed the night-vision periscope from her spy belt. Through its lens she scanned the area around the house for any sign of life.

"No one here," she reported. "Maybe Spot was

right. Maybe it is a trap. What time is it, anyway?"

"Eleven thirty and fifteen minutes," Zeke reported. He still hadn't gotten the hang of Earth time.

"Well, either no one is here yet or they're spying on me spying on them," said Cassie.

"Remain in position," said Zeke.

Cassie stifled a yawn and settled her back against the trunk of the willow tree to wait. Tired as she was, there was no danger of her falling asleep. The thundering of her heart was enough to keep anyone awake.

The seconds ticked by slowly. Cassie jumped at every rustling leaf, every creaking branch, every sound, however slight. When the walkie-talkie crackled in her hand, she nearly jumped out of her skin.

"It is midnight and five minutes," reported Zeke.

"Great!" said Cassie, jumping to her feet. "I'm leaving."

"No, Cassie!" Zeke said sternly.

Cassie moaned. Her worst fear was about to come true.

"Zeke, don't say it," she begged. "Please."

"Sorry, Cassie. You have got to try it just once. It is knock twice, count four, knock thrice, count six, knock twice."

"Are you crazy? What if someone answers the door?"

12

"Tell them that you are my representative. Ask them what they want."

"What if they grab me? What if they kidnap me or something?"

For a moment there was silence on the other end.

"Zeke?"

"You have a materializer disk," said the Triminican. "You can get out anytime you want to."

Cassie fingered the golden disk in the inside pocket of her jacket and smiled. The Triminicans had no need for cars or trains or airplanes. They traveled two ways: by spaceship and by materializer disk. There were thousands of the pancake-like objects in boxes on Zeke's spaceship. Zeke had given one to Cassie tonight for a quick getaway. She could throw the disk and disappear in a matter of seconds. But it was useless if someone opened the door and grabbed her or surprised her from behind.

"Come on, Cassie. Please," said Zeke. "This is important. We have to find out who these people are. Besides, Spot and I will rescue you if you get into trouble."

"Spies are brave, spies are brave, spies are brave." Over and over, Cassie whispered the words to herself as she approached the house. When she reached the front steps, she flipped the high-beam light on the ray gun and quickly scanned the area. The steps were coated with

13

dust, no footprints anywhere. Cassie raised the light long enough to scan the door. No smudges on the doorknob. No one had been inside this house for a very long time. Cassie shut off the light and, taking a deep breath, climbed the stairs.

She stared at the massive door for a long time, her breath coming out in short little gasps. "Okay, this is it," she whispered into the walkie-talkie. Then, clutching the materializer disk in her other hand, she knocked on the door. Twice.

Then she counted to four.

She knocked three times.

And counted to six.

She knocked twice.

And held her breath and waited.

But nothing happened. The door didn't open with a creak. There were no shuffling sounds inside the house. Nothing. With a sigh of relief, Cassie turned around and walked back down the steps.

She did not see the eyes peering out at her from behind a dust-coated pane of glass.

CHAPTER

"I'm *really* leaving now," Cassie whispered into the walkie-talkie as she tucked the ray gun back into her pocket.

"Circle the house once before you leave," Zeke's voice came back at her.

"Come on, Zeke. I'm tired. And this place is creepy enough from the front," Cassie complained.

But even as she whined into the walkie-talkie, she knew that she would do anything to help her friend. And she knew that Zeke was right. She couldn't leave before checking the whole house.

Cassie began circling. The dead leaves crunching beneath her feet were so loud that she kept stopping, half expecting someone to creep up behind her. As she neared the back corner of the house, she suddenly had the feeling that she was being watched. She had to protect herself.

"Zeke," she whispered into the walkie-talkie. "I'm going around to the back now. I'm shutting

you off and putting you in my pocket so I can hold the ray gun in one hand and the disk in the other."

"No," crackled Zeke's voice. "Do not cut off contact. . . . "

Cassie ignored him and shut off the walkie-talkie. Helping her friend was one thing, endangering her own life was another. With the ray gun set to scream at the push of a button and the materializer disk coordinates set for her bedroom, Cassie turned the corner into what she knew would be the darkest place she had ever been. Everyone knew that even the moon didn't shine behind the house at the end of Whisper Wind Lane.

Cassie saw the light the moment she turned the corner. It was a thin but very steady stream pouring out of a basement window. She didn't know whether to laugh out loud, run screaming into the night, or breathe a sigh of relief. There was someone inside! Or something! Or many somethings!

Swiftly Cassie pocketed the materializer disk and crouched down next to the window, which had been opened as far as it would go. Dropping silently to the ground, she discovered that if she lay in the dirt on her stomach with her cheek pressed against the sill, she could just see inside. And what she saw made her gasp.

There were several dozen people inside the

house. They were sitting and standing, milling about and talking. There were children and adults, men and women. Where had all these people come from? How had they gotten into the basement of the house? And what did they want with Zeke? Cassie was no longer frightened. She was burning up with curiosity, all her spy senses alert.

The people seemed ordinary enough. There was nothing particularly suspicious about them . . . or was there? Cassie couldn't quite put her finger on just what was bothering her about their appearance. And then suddenly it hit her. It was the hair! Every single person in the room, large or small, male or female, had a glorious mane of hair in one vibrant color or another. There were no balding men, no graying women, no mousy shades of brown. There was only pitch black, pure white, or corn yellow hair—all perfectly straight or perfectly curled. No frizzies, even.

Cassie couldn't hear what the people were saying. Only a dull murmur leaked out of the basement window. She fumbled in her spy belt for the listening device, then quickly clamped it to the sill. She slipped the earphones on. The device definitely magnified the sound, but it didn't help much. Now it sounded like a dull roar. There were simply too many people speaking at once.

Suddenly the noise stopped, and everyone

scrambled for a seat on one of the many metal chairs scattered around the room. Cassie's eyes drifted to the one person still standing, a man who looked to be in his mid-forties or maybe his fifties. Cassie couldn't tell—mainly because he had a full head of the brightest red hair Cassie had ever seen.

The man stood quietly at the end of the room, where all the chairs faced, his arms extended, his palms up. One by one everybody else extended their arms in the same gesture. Strange, thought Cassie. Something about the scene looked familiar. She racked her brain. Where had she seen that gesture before?

Cassie could hear everything the red-haired man said. He stood and spoke with the bearing of a leader.

"It appears our guest of honor will not be making an appearance tonight," he said.

No one said a word. But Cassie felt the wave of disappointment that washed across the room.

"We will, of course, continue to send invitations," said the red-haired man. "But as you know, there are no guarantees that we will ever be able to make contact."

This time Cassie heard several people groan. The man held up his hands to silence the crowd.

"I realize that some of you have traveled a great distance and may be forced to return to your homes without satisfaction. But I urge you

to remain here for two more days. After that . . . "
The man let his voice trail off.

After that, what? thought Cassie. Finish your
sentence.

But there didn't seem to be any need for the
man to continue. Everyone in the room knew
what he meant.

A hand shot up in the air, and the man beckoned for the person to speak. A woman with
deep blue-black hair stood up and asked a question. At least Cassie thought it was a question
from the way the woman's voice went up on the
last word. But there was really no way of know-
ing. Because not only was the woman not speaking English, she wasn't speaking any language
that Cassie had ever heard before. And Cassie
had heard nearly all of them at one time or another from her father, who taught languages at
the university.

"Speak in English!" snapped the red-haired
man.

The woman lowered her head for a moment—
perhaps in shame, perhaps to translate in her
mind—and then spoke again.

"Perhaps we need to be a bit more persua-
sive," she said.

"What do you suggest?" asked the man. "I am
open to any and all ideas."

"We should approach him directly," said the
woman.

The leader shook his head. "That would be far too dangerous," he said.

"Not if we do it out in the open," called a voice from the back of the room.

"Explain," said the leader.

A young man in the back of the room stood up and spoke.

"I say we attend the science fair!"

Cassie was so stunned that she made a little sound in her throat. It was a small sound, a cross between a gasp and a gulp. But it was loud enough. In one swift motion the person closest to the window rose and, sliding his hand through the window opening, grasped Cassie's hand. Before she could stop herself, Cassie screamed.

It was a mistake.

An entire roomful of heads swiveled in Cassie's direction. Then everybody rose as one and raced toward the window. Cassie yanked her hand as hard as she could and freed it from the grasp of the man inside.

Cassie ran. And ran . . . and ran . . . and ran. All the way to the end of Whisper Wind Lane. But when she stopped to catch her breath and, if there was time, to throw the materializer disk, Cassie was shocked to hear nothing behind her. No footsteps, no voices, nothing. She spun around. All was still. Okay, so they were letting her go—for now. But she couldn't go to the ship. What if they followed her? They probably already knew where it was because one of them had left the note. But still . . . Cassie's head was spinning. She was tired and frightened and cold. Maybe if she went home and called Zeke. No. There was no telephone on the spaceship.

Finally Cassie just activated the materializer disk and threw it. It arced high and wide and then ricocheted back to her. At the exact moment it would have crashed into her body, the disk spun out and began circling Cassie. Faster and faster it circled, leaving a trail of brilliant, sparkling light in its path.

Moments later, Cassie crashed onto her bedroom floor. She sat up and rubbed her bruised knee. She was going to have to practice those landings!

CHAPTER

4

When Cassie woke on Sunday morning, her first thought was of Zeke. After her crash landing the night before, she had remembered that she could contact Zeke by walkie-talkie. But much to her dismay, she couldn't find the spy device anywhere. She must have dropped it in midflight. Zeke and Spot were probably very worried by now. And she had to tell them about the red-haired man and his friends as soon as possible. She would race over to the spaceship as soon as she finished breakfast. Even better, she thought as she slipped into a sweatsuit, she would grab a donut and eat it on the way.

As Cassie hurried down the stairs, the smell of pancakes and bacon wafted up to greet her. Maybe she would sit down and eat after all. Sunday breakfasts were Mr. Williams's specialty.

But the happy family scene that awaited Cassie in the kitchen made her freeze in her tracks. Everyone sat around the large oak table, talking and munching on Mr. Williams's famous banana pancakes. There was Mr. and Mrs. Williams, Cassie's little brother Simon, Ben O'Brien, and Zeke. *Ben O'Brien? Zeke?* Oh no! thought Cassie. She had completely forgotten that Ben was coming over so they could fix the solar system. But what was Zeke doing there?

"Uh . . . good morning," Cassie said, staring at them all in confusion.

"Well, good morning, sleepyhead!" said Mr. Williams cheerily. "Better hurry up or all the pancakes will be gone. Your friend here has a huge appetite."

Somehow Cassie assumed he was talking about Ben. But when she sat down at the table, she saw that Zeke had an enormous stack of pancakes on his plate, floating in half a gallon of maple syrup. She smiled across the table at the Triminican. He grinned back at her and winked. Ben was so busy eating that he never looked up from his plate.

"Um, I'm sorry I slept so late," Cassie said as she helped herself to pancakes.

"Okay by me," Ben said, shoveling food into his mouth.

"You must have had a late night," said Zeke, a devilish glint in his eye.

"Uh, yeah," said Cassie, grinning. She caught her mother looking at her and corrected herself.

"Well, not a late night, but kind of a long one,"

she said carefully. "I had this really weird dream."

Cassie took a bite of her pancake and chewed thoughtfully. She wanted to tell Zeke everything right then and there. But she had to be careful.

"What was your dream about, Cass?" Simon chirped.

Cassie smiled at her little brother. Sometimes she wondered what she would do without him. She chose her words carefully.

"I was . . . uh . . . using my spy kit to spy on some people, and they saw me, and . . . they grabbed me . . . and I ran away and dropped my walkie-talkie."

Cassie watched Zeke's fake eyebrows lift so high they practically blended into the wig he was wearing. It reminded her of what he looked like when she first saw him. He had been hairless, with foot-long fingernails, extending his arms toward her with the palms up *exactly the same way the man at the meeting had last night*, talking in a clicking language that sounded *just like the language the woman spoke last night*. Cassie's fork slipped out of her hand and into a puddle of maple syrup on her plate.

"Cassie—are you all right?" her mother asked.

"Uh, fine, Mom. Why?"

"You look pale, dear. And you seem so nervous," said Mrs. Williams, looking concerned.

"I . . . uh . . . am nervous, Mom," said Cassie, standing up from the table. "I'm nervous that

Ben and I won't have enough time to finish our project. Come on, Ben, let's go!"

"But I haven't finished eating!" Ben complained.

"There isn't enough time for that," Cassie snapped, heading for the garage, where their science project lay in pieces.

"Sure there is," Ben whined. "Especially since Zeke showed up to help us. He's a whiz in science."

So that was the reason no one had questioned why Zeke was there.

"Cassie knows I love science," Zeke said quickly. "I told you she asked me to come over and help you."

Zeke rose from the table and joined Cassie. "Let me have a look at what you have done so far," he said. "Ben, meet us in the garage when you have finished eating."

Zeke followed Cassie out to the garage, pausing at the door to turn and thank Cassie's parents for breakfast. Once outside, Cassie quickly filled Zeke in on what had happened the night before. She talked a mile a minute, rushing toward the end so she could ask Zeke the question burning in her mind.

"Zeke, what does this mean to you?" she asked, holding her arms out, palms upward.

"It is a Triminican greeting," said Zeke.

"That's what I thought!" said Cassie triumphantly. "Zeke, I think those people were from your planet!"

"Cassie—that is impossible!"

"But that was the way the man greeted the group last night," said Cassie. "And they all did it back!"

"I am sure it is not as uncommon a gesture as you think, Cassie."

"Well, how about that weird language that woman spoke?" said Cassie insistently. "I mean, I didn't realize it at first, but it had all these clicking sounds in it—just like Triminican!"

"Cassie, as much as I would like to believe you, those 'clicking sounds,' as you call them, appear in numerous languages that I know of."

Zeke tapped on his fingers as he made a list: "Mercutian, Dilariuz, Coututian, and even some of the dialects of . . . "

"Stop!" cried Cassie, laughing.

"I see I have made my point," said Zeke.

"The only point you've made," said Cassie, "is that a lot of the languages in the galaxy you come from have clicking sounds in them. Languages on Earth do not!"

"What are you guys talking about?" Ben O'Brien interrupted, appearing behind them.

"The science project, of course," said Cassie quickly.

"The science project is over there," said Ben, pointing to the far end of the garage.

Before Ben could say another word, Cassie grabbed Zeke's arm and dragged him over to the table, where charred bits of metal and plaster of paris were all that were left of the inner half of the solar system. The outer planets had somehow managed to remain intact, although the rings of Saturn looked more like triangles.

For a full five minutes Zeke examined the damaged planets and the fried electrical wiring without saying anything. Then suddenly he was issuing orders: Cassie get me this, Ben go for that, mix more plaster, twist this wire, paint this, glue that. Zeke then fell silent, focusing on the solar system with such concentration that Cassie was suddenly struck by how easy school on Earth must be for him.

Exactly two hours after they had started, the solar system was completed. Zeke had even managed to wire the sun to glow.

"It's beautiful, Zeke. Even better than what we had yesterday," said Cassie. She smiled at her friend. "Thank you."

"Yeah, thanks, Zeke," said Ben, polite for once. "It really does look a lot better than what we did. You're not telling anyone you helped us, are you?"

"It will be our secret," said Zeke. He turned to Cassie. "I believe we have someplace to go right now?"

Cassie couldn't believe it! She had almost forgotten about T.O.E.

28

"Yeah, right!" she said. "Well, bye, Ben. We've got to go. See you tomorrow. I'll bring the project to school. My mom will drive me." Cassie kept up a steady stream of babble as she grabbed Ben's arm and tried to walk him out of the garage. But Ben wouldn't budge.

"Where are you going?" he asked suspiciously.

"Oh, someplace stupid," said Cassie. "You wouldn't be interested."

"Sure I would," said Ben. "Come on, tell me."

Cassie groaned. Ever since they had tricked Ben into helping them get rid of a real spy who was following Zeke, Ben had become very nosy. But there was absolutely no way Cassie and Zeke were going to let him spy with them. There was too much danger of his discovering Zeke's secret. And Ben O'Brien was not to be trusted.

"We are going to hear Cassie's father lecture at the university," Zeke said quickly.

Good one, thought Cassie, breathing a sigh of relief.

"Oh," said Ben. "What's he lecturing on?"

"Grammatical structuring of the Mandarin language," said Zeke. "Would you like to join us?"

Ben's face went completely blank, and Cassie knew that Zeke had done it. Ben was out the garage door and down the block in less than thirty seconds. Thirty seconds after that, Cassie and Zeke materialized behind the house at the end of Whisper Wind Lane.

Cassie had to admit that the old house was far less spooky in the light of day. But the knowledge of what she had seen the night before made her almost as nervous as the possibility of ghosts.

The two spies returned to the scene of Cassie's discovery. The basement window was closed and locked. They peered inside, but the room looked empty. Cassie searched the grounds but could not find her walkie-talkie anywhere.

"This is weird, Zeke," she told her friend. "It's almost like it never happened."

"Let us go inside," said Zeke.

"What? No! Absolutely not."

"You do not really think this house is haunted, do you, Cassie? Not after what you saw last night."

"No, of course not," said Cassie defensively. "Unless, of course, those people were ghosts."

"Triminican ghosts?"

"I thought you said there was no way they could be from your planet."

"Correct," said Zeke. "This solar system is not charted by our people."

Cassie looked at her friend. His words were saying no, but his eyes were saying, Wow—people from my own planet!

"Okay, let's go inside!" she said. "Even if they were ghosts, everyone knows ghosts don't come out in the daytime."

The two of them walked to the front of the house and climbed the dusty stairs to the door.

"Should we knock?" Cassie asked.

"Very funny," said Zeke.

"I'm serious, Zeke. Maybe we should try the code again."

Zeke dug into his pocket and pulled out the rumpled piece of stationery. He read from it.

"Knock twice, count four, knock thrice, count six, knock twice."

Cassie tried the code. The two spies held their breath and waited for someone—or something—to answer the door.

Nothing.

This time Zeke tried.

Nothing.

Cassie took a deep breath and, ignoring the pounding in her ears, turned the dust-covered doorknob. With a creak the door opened, and the two spies slipped inside.

The house was a mess. Cobwebs and dust covered everything. The few pieces of furniture were from another century. But they weren't priceless antiques, just relics with broken coils and jutting springs. Splintered pieces of wood lay everywhere.

The basement door groaned when Cassie opened it, and the worn stairs threatened to give way beneath her feet. But together she and Zeke moved forward, down, down into the dank and darkened basement where Cassie had seen the secret meeting the night before.

When they reached the bottom of the stairs, Cassie gasped. Not only were there no people—there were no chairs. And the electricity didn't work when she flipped the switch.

"Zeke, I don't understand. I swear the room was lit up. And there were at least forty chairs here."

"I believe you, Cassie," Zeke said sadly. "But let us examine the facts. There is no longer any sign of a meeting. The people you saw last night are long gone."

Cassie and the Spy from Outer Space climbed back up the stairs and left the house at the end of Whisper Wind Lane. They never looked back. If they had, they would have seen a small tunnel door at the base of the steps creak open—and a head with bright red hair lean out and watch them leave.

CHAPTER

By eight A.M. on Monday morning, the gymnasium at Hillsdale Elementary School was humming with excitement. Classes had been canceled for the morning so that everyone could attend the science fair. There were children and teachers and parents. Younger brothers and older sisters. Aunts and uncles and grandparents and, of course, the favorite librarian. Though the fair did not officially begin until 8:30, everyone was there already. And those who were not would have trouble getting in the door.

In a corner of the room, immediately to the right of the Fifth Grade sign, Cassie and Ben struggled with the wilting rings of Saturn that had been damaged in transport. They were proving more difficult to fix than Cassie imagined, but she cheered herself up by listening to Marilee Tischler as she worked.

Marilee was trying to explain the molecule-splitting experiment that she and Zeke had created to a group of parents. She clearly had no idea what she was talking about. She kept pronouncing the word "molecules" as "*molercules*" and giggling whenever anyone asked her a question, saying, "Oh, Zeke explains it so much better than I do." For once Marilee wasn't making Cassie sick with her sugar-sweet voice. She was making a fool of herself!

Cassie had just straightened out the last ring of Saturn and sent it spinning when a familiar voice called her name.

"Oh, look—there she is!" Mrs. Williams appeared with Simon in tow. They oohed and aahed over the solar system, and then Cassie's father showed up and oohed some more, and then the three of them went to look at the other experiments, and that was when Cassie saw *him*. He was leaning against the wall, staring straight at Cassie. A shiver ran down her spine, and she froze. She didn't want to make a move until she knew exactly what she was going to do.

But she didn't have to make a decision at all. Suddenly there was a tap on her shoulder, and Zeke was standing next to her.

"How is the solar system?" he asked.

Cassie turned as casually as she could.

"He's here," she said, keeping her mouth in a frozen smile.

"What? Who?"

"The leader of T.O.E.," Cassie whispered. "He's

34

leaning against the wall behind me. He has really bright red hair; that's why I saw him. I swear it's him."

Zeke looked over Cassie's shoulder.

"I do not see anyone with red hair, Cassie," he said.

"What?"

Cassie whirled around. The man was gone.

"I swear he was right there, Zeke."

"Zekephlon," said a voice, and Cassie watched all the color drain from Zeke's face at the Triminican form of his name. Slowly her friend turned and faced the red-haired man, who extended his arms, palms upward, and repeated Zeke's name.

"Can I help you, sir?" asked Zeke, no emotion in his voice at all. Cassie was sure he had learned that trick at the spy academy.

"You are Zekephlon?" asked the man.

"My name is Zeke," said Zeke calmly. "Who are you?"

"I am Cardeklpe," clicked the man.

"That is an odd name," said Zeke.

A smirk spread across the red-haired man's face. He looked around at the clusters of students and parents.

"I understand," he said. "Perhaps we should speak outside."

"About what?" asked Zeke.

Cassie had no idea what the man said next because he said it in Triminican. But there was no mistaking the look of amazement that briefly flickered across Zeke's face.

"Perhaps we *had* better step outside," said Zeke.

The man nodded and turned to leave the gymnasium. Zeke beckoned for Cassie to join them and then followed the red-haired man out of the school building.

In a small alcove right outside the front door, Zeke confronted the man.

"All right. Who are you, and what do you want?"

"As I told you, my name is Cardeklpe. I am the leader of the organization known as T.O.E., and we need your help." He pointed at Cassie suspiciously. "She is not one of us, is she?"

"One of who?" asked Zeke.

"I recognize her from your afternoon visit to the house," said the red-haired man. "I assume she was also the female at the window that night."

"What do you mean you recognize me from that afternoon?" Cassie exclaimed. "We looked everywhere. No one was inside the house!"

The man did not respond.

"If you saw us, why did you not reveal yourselves?" asked Zeke.

"To be honest, we did not know what you looked like, and we were thrown by the presence of the girl," the man admitted.

Zeke studied the red-haired man. "You have not said what you want," he said.

"I do not understand your attitude," said the man. "There is no need for you to be suspicious."

"I think my attitude is quite understandable," said Zeke. "You leave a threatening note and then grab at my friend. Why should I trust you?"

"The note was not intended as a threat," the man said pleasantly. "It was an invitation."

"Do all your invitations say 'or else' on them?" asked Cassie.

"We had to make certain that Zekephlon would attend. We could think of no other way," the man explained. "And we only grabbed at you because we did not know who you were and feared that you would reveal our location to the authorities."

"Which authorities?" asked Cassie.

The man seemed to feel as if he had done enough talking to Cassie for one day. He ignored her last question and focused on Zeke.

"We desire an audience with Mirac," he said simply.

"Mirac is not here."

"We know that. But he will be returning from the Hawaiian volcano today."

Cassie saw Zeke start. Mirac and Inora had been unable to estimate when they would return.

"It is of the utmost importance that we speak with him," said the red-haired man. "Tell him that we can help. But the offer is only good for forty-eight hours."

"What do you mean, you can help?" asked Zeke.

"I will say nothing further until I speak with Mirac," said the man. "Remember to tell him the offer is only good for forty-eight hours."

Zeke stared at the red-haired man a moment.

"We will see," Zeke said finally. He turned on his heels and walked swiftly back to the school building, letting the door slam shut behind him. The red-haired man winked at Cassie, then headed off in the opposite direction, away from the school. Cassie stood still for a minute and then raced after Zeke. But when she reached the door, she found it blocked by Ben O'Brien.

"Who was that?" he said. "And who's Mirac? And what's he doing in a volcano in Hawaii?"

CHAPTER 7

Cassie stared at Ben and tried to remain calm. What would Zeke do in this situation? she asked herself.

Change the conversation.

"Ben, what are you doing out here? Who's guarding our solar system? Who's explaining it to everyone?"

"Who's Mirac?" Ben repeated.

"Who?" said Cassie.

"And why exactly was he in a volcano in Hawaii?" asked Ben. "I didn't quite catch all of the conversation."

I didn't quite catch all of the conversation? thought Cassie. Since when did Ben talk like this? Was nosiness actually making him smarter? Cassie thought quickly. She didn't know how much of the conversation Ben had overheard. But if he hadn't heard everything, she had a chance.

"Oh," she said as casually as possible, "You mean Mark. That's Zeke's father, my uncle. He's in Hawaii on business. That's why Zeke is staying with us."

"Who was that man?" Ben demanded. "And what is really going on here? You know, the more I think about it, there *is* something really strange about Zeke. I always thought so."

"Now, look, Ben. I don't know why you're spying on us. But this is ridiculous. We have to get back inside."

She brushed past Ben and into the noisy gymnasium. Ben followed, shouting questions at the back of her head. Cassie ignored him. Eventually she would have to figure out how to get Ben off their back, but for now she figured she could get lost in the chaos of the fair. Or maybe Ben could get lost while she tended to the solar system.

And then Cassie heard something that was music to her ears.

"Benjamin!"

"Oh, hi, Mom."

"Benjamin, where is your solar system? I've been looking all over for it."

Cassie turned around with her sweetest smile. "Hi, Mrs. O'Brien. I'm Cassie Williams. Can I walk you to our project?"

Mrs. O'Brien, a giant female version of Ben, looked thrilled.

"Well, thank you, Cassie," she said, hooking one arm in Cassie's arm and the other in her son's. The three of them walked over to the Fifth

Grade sign like one big happy family—except for the fact that Ben kept glaring at Cassie behind his mother's back.

Cassie and Ben got an *A* on their science experiment. Zeke and Marilee got an *A* also, although Ms. Grayson kind of accused them of cheating until Zeke gave a lengthy, detailed explanation of molecular properties. Then Ms. Grayson looked all flustered and said that Zeke should really skip a few grades, sciencewise.

Lunchtime signaled the end of the science fair and the return to classes that afternoon. As soon as the noon bell rang, Cassie grabbed Zeke and yanked him to a corner of the gym.

"We've got trouble," she said.

"Tell me about it," said Zeke. Cassie couldn't help but grin. Zeke had picked up that expression on Earth.

"I'm not just talking about that red-haired guy with the weird name," said Cassie. "I'm talking about Ben. He overheard us."

"Oh no!" Zeke exclaimed. "What are we going to do?"

"I don't know," said Cassie. "Can we go to the ship for lunch? Maybe Spot will have some ideas."

Zeke nodded thoughtfully, looking past Cassie. Suddenly his eyes widened.

"Uh-oh, bully advancing!" Zeke grabbed Cassie's arm, and the two of them flew through the gymnasium doors and outside, where they raced to the back of the school. Cassie checked to make certain no one was watching while Zeke dug for the emergency materializer disk he always kept hidden in his shoe. Then, punching in the appropriate coordinates, Zeke threw the disk and took Cassie's hand. The disk spun out and back, trailing its circle of sparkling light.

Just as the two spies were enveloped in light, Ben O'Brien appeared. He lunged for the cloud of sparkles. But he was too late and found himself facedown in the dirt. Cassie and Zeke never even knew Ben had seen them vanish.

A moment later, in the field just outside of town, Cassie and the Spy from Outer Space materialized. Quickly Zeke deactivated the invisibility shield, and from inside the ship, Spot lowered the staircase. When they boarded, Cassie and Zeke gasped in unison. Standing there, waiting to greet them, were Mirac and Inora. They were home from Hawaii.

Just like the red-haired man had said they would be.

CHAPTER

8

Cardeklpe had been right. Mirac and Inora had finished mining the iridium they needed from the volcano and returned to Hillsdale.

Zeke filled his parents in on the events of the past few days. When he finished, neither Mirac nor Inora said anything for a very long time. The silence was so thick, Cassie felt she could reach out and touch it. She squirmed uncomfortably in her seat while Mirac studied the crumpled note that Zeke had saved.

Finally the older Triminican spoke.

"The next time he contacts you, bring him to the ship," he instructed his son.

"What?" cried Cassie.

Mirac looked at her sternly.

"I mean, I know this is none of my business, but do you really think that's such a good idea?" she said softly.

"Of course it is a good idea," Mirac said simply. "For one thing, he speaks our language. And I am

44

very curious to know how he happened to learn it."

"And he did leave the note on the table," Inora added. "So he has been aboard this ship already. Still, Mirac, I must agree with Cassie. This man does sound more violent than most Triminicans. Extreme caution should be exercised."

"Agreed," said Mirac, standing up from his seat.

"It is time for the two of you to return to the school building, and I have much to do," he said dismissively. "The iridium must be converted to fuel, and the robot and I must attempt to solve the gravity problem. Return here after school, preferably with the leader of that group."

Zeke knew better than to argue with his father. With a look at Cassie, he grabbed his school-books and lowered the staircase. Outside, as the two friends prepared to materialize back at school, Cassie stopped Zeke from throwing the disk.

"Zeke, let's walk to school. I have a lot to ask you. And this may be our last day together."

"Very well," said Zeke, pocketing the material-izer disk, "although I doubt very much that this will be our last day here."

"What do you mean? After Mirac puts the fuel in, you can go, right?"

"Cassie, you keep forgetting that the last time we took off, we had an adequate fuel supply, yet something else pulled us back into this planet's gravitational field. We cannot leave until Mirac and the robot locate the source of that problem."

Cassie didn't know whether to be thrilled that her friend would be staying a little longer or to be incredibly worried. Between the gravity problem, the red-haired man, and Ben O'Brien, life on Earth was getting very dangerous for Zeke and his family.

"What are we going to do about Ben?" Cassie asked.

"I do not know exactly," said Zeke. "I suppose we will have to wait and see just how persistent he is going to be."

Persistent became Ben's middle name. All afternoon he followed Cassie around, asking questions and trying to eavesdrop when she talked to Zeke. He knew better than to bother Zeke directly. When the alien first arrived at school, Ben made the mistake of challenging him to a fight. And although Zeke always preferred *not* to fight, Ben now knew better than to anger him.

Cassie managed to wiggle out of the tricky questions Ben threw her way. But she knew that she would not be able to withstand his constant badgering for long. She couldn't believe it, but by the end of the day she was actually hoping that her best friend would be able to return to his planet soon. Before Ben O'Brien ruined everything.

After school Cassie and Zeke walked back to

the house at the end of Whisper Wind Lane to look for the red-haired man.

They were about to use the knocking code when Cassie had the sudden feeling they were being watched. Turning quickly, she saw a flash of blue.

"Zeke." She stopped her friend from going in the house. "Ben's following us."

Zeke turned around swiftly.

"I do not see him. Are you sure?"

"I'm positive. I saw his blue windbreaker. He's behind that tree back there."

"Let us get out of here," said Zeke.

The two friends made a U-turn and, pretending that they did not see Ben, walked back the way they had come.

"Where should we go? We cannot return to the ship with Ben following us. And we need to find Cardeklpe," Zeke said, clicking the name expertly.

"How about my house?" asked Cassie.

"All right."

After a snack at the Williamses', Cassie and Zeke felt sure they had ditched Ben. Using a materializer disk, they returned to the ship. When they clambered up the stairs, they were shocked to find Mirac and Inora deep in conversation with the red-haired man. Mirac saw them, stood up from his chair, and motioned for them to join him.

"Zekephlon," said Mirac. "I would like for you to be formally introduced to Cardeklpe. He is the leader of a group known as T.O.E., which stands for Triminicans on Earth. It appears that there are many of us stranded on this planet. And thanks to our friend here, we are all going home!"

Cassie stayed on board the spaceship until dinnertime, watching and listening to the Triminicans make plans. They talked a mile a minute in a mixture of English and Triminican technological terminology that Cassie could not understand. But by the time she left, Cassie had a pretty good idea of what was going on. And what was going on, she thought sadly as Zeke walked her back to her house, was simple: Zeke was going home. Tomorrow.

According to Cardeklpe, a Triminican ship had crashed on Earth two years ago. It was broken beyond repair. With no way of returning home, the Triminicans had scattered over the planet. They wore wigs and clipped their fingernails. They stuffed rocks into their pockets to keep themselves grounded on Earth. And they integrated themselves into all walks of life. But they kept in touch, always. Because as much as they liked Earth, they wanted to make certain that if the chance arose, they could return home.

The Triminican network extended far and wide. They kept track of UFO sightings and anything else mysterious that might link them with other Triminicans or with anyone else from their galaxy who could help them get home. But up until this point, all of their leads had led to dashed hopes and nothing more.

Then came the UFO sightings in Hillsdale. And only a few weeks after that, the report about the mysterious iridium mining in the Hawaiian volcano. The alarm went out, and Triminicans flocked to Hillsdale, where they had been living in a series of tunnels beneath the house at the end of Whisper Wind Lane.

"So how come only forty-one Triminicans are leaving with you tomorrow?" Cassie asked her friend as they walked across the field. "I thought there were two hundred on the ship when it crashed."

"There are many reasons," Zeke explained. "In two years a lot can happen. Cardeklpe reports that some of our people died and others choose to remain behind."

"Really?" said Cassie. "More than a hundred Triminicans are choosing to stay on Earth?"

"Actually, no," Zeke admitted. "They only figured out the location of the ship a few days ago. By the time word got out to everyone, too much time had gone by." He sighed. "Unfortunately, without any materializer disks left, many people could not get to Hillsdale in time. And that is the main reason that many Triminicans will not travel back with us: they simply cannot get here by takeoff."

"So postpone takeoff!" said Cassie triumphantly. "That way you can stay here longer, too!"

Zeke smiled. "I would really like that, Cassie. But it is not that simple."

"The gravity thing, right?" said Cassie.

Zeke nodded. "You understood more than I thought. I am impressed."

"All I understood is that the planets have to be lined up in a certain way for you to get back to Triminica."

"Right. One of our people has been charting this for her entire time on Earth."

"And you have to leave tomorrow," said Cassie sadly.

"Yes," said Zeke. "Tomorrow night at 6:39 the planets will be aligned correctly for us to break the galaxy's gravitational pull. This will not occur again for six months and two days."

"And that's why the guy with the name I can't pronounce has been such a pest," said Cassie.

"You are correct again," said Zeke. "Once he learned that Mirac would be returning, he knew there was a chance. I guess our suspicions about him were wrong. If not for him, my family and I would not be returning home."

51

"Hey—we're spies!" said Cassie, grinning at her friend. "It's our job to be suspicious."

The two spies had arrived at the front of Cassie's house.

"Do you want to come in for dinner?" Cassie asked.

"I cannot," said Zeke. "I must return to the ship and assist Mirac. That is our agreement. That is the only way he will allow me to attend school tomorrow."

"It was nice of him to agree to that," said Cassie.

"I will go to the principal and tell him that I am leaving, so you do not get in trouble," said Zeke.

"Thank you," Cassie said softly. She could feel herself getting sad already.

"I kind of wish I could go with you tomorrow," she said, smiling at her friend.

"I wish that also, Cassie," said Zeke. "It would be wonderful to show you my galaxy. Unfortunately, even if we could get your parents' permission *and* Mirac and Inora's permission, it would not be possible."

Cassie laughed. "Yeah, right. I can just see it. 'Mom, can I go to Zeke's house for dinner?' 'Where does he live?' 'Oh, this other planet in another galaxy. . . . ' "

Zeke started laughing also, and for a moment the two friends forgot that they were sad.

"But I am afraid it is even more complicated than that," said Zeke. "You see, we do not fly straight to Triminica or to any planet in the galaxy without going through one of a number of transport stations."

"Kind of like customs at our airports?" asked Cassie.

"Yes," said Zeke. "Kind of. And . . . well . . . the truth is that with the additional weight of all our people, we do not have enough fuel to return to the transport station closest to Triminica. We will have to land on Station 712."

"That's bad?" asked Cassie.

"It is run by the Delphs," Zeke explained.

"And *that's* bad?"

Zeke nodded his head. "That is bad. The Delphs are a violent, greedy race of beings. They are the bullies of our universe."

"Oh no!" cried Cassie. "Will you be in danger?"

"No," said Zeke. "But you would be if you came with us. Unaccompanied minors whose parents do not meet them at Station 712 are sent to the orphan colony planet. And from there you would have a hard time returning home."

"The orphan colony planet?" Cassie exclaimed. "You're kidding!"

"I am afraid not," said Zeke.

"That's awful," said Cassie, shivering at the thought.

"I know," Zeke admitted. "Everything I told

you about how wonderful Triminica is, is true!" he added, anxious for Cassie to believe him. "It is just that the whole galaxy is not as great as it could be."

"That's okay, Zeke. But I don't think I'll visit you this time, just the same. Okay?"

"Okay," said Zeke, smiling fondly at her. With nothing else to say, the two spies just stood there grinning at each other.

"Well, I will see you tomorrow," said Zeke at last.

"Right. Tomorrow," said Cassie, wondering what she was going to do in Hillsdale without her best friend and spying partner.

Neither Cassie nor Zeke saw Ben O'Brien lurking behind a tree in the yard of the house next door.

CHAPTER

10

True to his word, Zeke went to the principal's office first thing in the morning. He took Cassie with him and told Principal Levine he had to return home to be with his parents. Cassie hardly breathed the whole time Zeke talked. She was sure the principal was going to pick up the phone and call her mother to make sure Zeke was telling the truth. But that never happened, and soon Cassie was sitting in a classroom, worrying about orphan colonies and transport stations.

Cassie was amazed that Zeke wanted to spend his last day on Earth at Hillsdale Elementary School. But she was even more amazed at Ben's behavior. For the first time since the science fair, he didn't follow her around, he didn't ask questions. He actually sat still in classes. If Cassie had given it much thought, she would have figured something strange was going on. But she noticed it and forgot it. She was too busy thinking about other things.

After school Cassie and Zeke went to the mall so Zeke could play one last round of Laser Lunacy and eat one last corndog. They materialized back at the ship at six o'clock so Cassie could say good-bye to Mirac, Inora, and Spot. Liftoff was at exactly 6:39.

The ship was buzzing with excitement. To Cassie it was a sea of clicks and clacks. After two years on Earth, most of the Triminicans had not even bothered to take their wigs off on the ship. If not for the strange language, it could easily have been a group of humans, Cassie thought. She said her good-byes to everyone but Zeke, and her friend walked her to the ship's exit. Tearfully, Cassie stood gazing at the Triminicans milling about the ship.

"Cassie, it is six thirty and three minutes. You really must leave now," Zeke said softly.

"I know, I know," said Cassie. She put on her best doom-and-gloom voice. "Or I will spend my days on the orphan colony planet."

Zeke laughed.

"It has been a wonderful time," he said. "I will miss you."

Cassie opened her mouth to say good-bye, but when she spoke it was more like a shriek.

"BEN!"

"What?" cried Zeke, whirling around.

Ben O'Brien was entering the room from another part of the spaceship. Hearing Cassie cry his name, he turned around and dashed out the door. The two spies sprang into action, racing after him, in and out of rooms, down first one spiral staircase and then another, and then down yet another staircase to the storage area of the ship. Once there, they stood gasping for air, uncertain of where to look next.

"How did he . . . ," Cassie wheezed.

"I do not know . . . ," Zeke said back in short breaths. "But we have less than two minutes to find him."

"Let's split up!" said Cassie.

"No. You must leave the ship now!"

A crash from a room nearby sent the spies flying in the direction of the sound. They reached a door and tried to open it. It was locked from the inside. In a flash, Zeke whipped a small metal device from his pocket and shot zorcanian 6 at the lock. Instantly the lock melted into a puddle. The Triminican forced the door open, and he and Cassie burst inside.

Ben was standing in a corner. "What are you doing here?" Cassie yelled.

"Leave me alone!" Ben cried. "I want to go to outer space!"

"There is no time for this, Cassie," said Zeke frantically. "We have to get him—and you—off this ship right now!"

Zeke and Cassie both lunged at Ben, tackling him to the ground.

"Leave me alone," Ben bellowed again. "I'm staying."

"Ben, you're making a mistake," Cassie panted as she and Zeke began to drag the bully across the floor of the spaceship.

But it was too late. The engines roared, the ship lurched, and suddenly Cassie felt as if the world had dropped from under her. She, Zeke, and Ben all raced for the window—and watched the Earth grow small beneath them.

"WOW!" exclaimed Ben.

"AMAZING!" cried Cassie.

"Oh no," groaned Zeke, shaking his head and pacing back and forth while Cassie and Ben remained glued to the ship's window, watching the Earth gradually disappear from view.

"This is incredible!" Ben shouted, turning to grin at Cassie. "Definitely the absolute best thing that's ever happened to me."

"Me, too!" said Cassie, grinning back. Then she remembered what Zeke had told her about the orphan colony, and she felt all the color drain from her face.

"Ben, you shouldn't have done this," she said, turning to watch her Triminican friend pace.

"Oh yeah?" snapped Ben, still staring out the window. "Why not?"

"Just take it from me," said Cassie. "It was a mistake." She moved away from Ben and began pacing beside Zeke.

"Zeke, what should we do?" she asked, trying to keep the panic out of her voice.

"Zeke, what should we do?" Ben imitated Cassie in his most obnoxious whine.

"Shut up, Ben!" Cassie snapped.

"Don't tell me to shut up!" Ben snarled, turning away from the window. "You're just mad because you wanted to be the only one to ride on a spaceship."

Cassie stopped walking and faced Ben.

"I wasn't going to ride on a spaceship, Ben. This is an accident."

"Sure it is," said Ben. "So, where are we going?"

In one swift motion, Zeke crossed the room, grabbed Ben by the shoulders, and turned him around. He spoke softly, his face close to Ben's. But the anger and intensity in his voice frightened Cassie, who had come to know him so well.

"I do not know how you happened to be on this ship. But you have made the mistake of your life. We are returning to a place where you and Cassie, as unaccompanied minors, will be sent to the orphan colony planet. You will not like it there. I promise you that!"

Ben burst out laughing and tried to shrug Zeke's hands off his shoulders. But Zeke's grip held firm, and finally Ben gave up trying to get free.

"Lighten up, E.T.," Ben said. "Your threats don't scare me. Orphan colony. Right!" He started laughing again. Cassie watched, her heart pounding a mile a minute.

"I want an explanation," said Zeke. "How did you find the ship?"

"All right, all right," said Ben. "Just let go of me."

"After you explain."

Ben sighed.

"I've been following you," he said.

"We know that," said Zeke. "We did not lead you anywhere."

"That's not true," said Ben triumphantly. "I got better at hiding myself after you saw me follow you to the house that day. Last night I was hiding near Cassie's house. I followed you back here and saw the ship and everything. . . . Hey, loosen that grip, will you?"

"Continue."

"Okay, okay. I didn't know you were taking off. But I did know there was no way you were going to tell me anything. So I came back here today after school to snoop around. And the spaceship was here, and there were all these people getting on, and I just kind of mixed in with the crowd."

"And?" demanded Zeke.

"And that's it. I swear. I just got lucky." Ben squinted his eyes at Zeke and looked the Triminican up and down. "I can't believe you're an alien. I mean, I *can* believe it when I think about all the weird stuff you've done. But you look normal and all that."

Cassie watched the look of disgust that crossed Zeke's face. This is it, she thought, now Zeke's going to beat Ben up. But the Spy from Outer Space just shook his head, dropped his hands, and looked sadly at Cassie.

"You must not be seen by anyone," he explained to his friend. "No Triminican would want to harm you. But if word of your existence reaches the transport station, if anyone aboard this ship should accidentally tell the Delphs about you . . . " He did not finish his sentence.

Cassie nodded. "I understand," she said softly. "What do you want us to do?"

"Remain here," he said. "I must notify Mirac of this development. Perhaps there is still something that can be done."

"Like what?" asked Cassie.

Zeke shrugged his shoulders. "I do not know." He turned and left the room, closing the door behind him.

The second Zeke was out of view, Ben turned to Cassie, his face aglow. "Let's explore!"

"What? Ben, are you crazy? You heard what Zeke said."

"So what?" said Ben. "What's he going to do to me? Send me to his orphan colony?" Ben laughed and slapped his thigh. "Wooo—that's a good one. I wonder where he came up with that."

"He didn't make it up, Ben. We could be in real danger."

"Well, stay here if you want," said Ben. "I'm going to snoop around the ship."

"No, Ben, don't!" Cassie pleaded. But Ben ignored her. Cassie watched him run out the door, down the hall, and up a narrow spiral staircase. Within seconds he had disappeared from view.

Cassie was suddenly embarrassed that Ben was the only other human on board the ship. He was behaving like a jerk! She stared after the bully, wondering what a member of the Interstellar Spy Academy would do. Zeke was going to be furious when he returned and found that Ben was gone. Would Zeke blame her? Would he get in trouble with Mirac? Should she just go find Ben? Suddenly Cassie wished she hadn't left her spy belt at home.

Still, she *was* a super sleuth. Cautiously she leaned out the doorway and peered down the hall. It was empty. Taking a deep breath, Cassie slipped out of the small room. She raced down the hallway and up the spiral staircase. She was standing in the middle of the hallway, wondering where to look first, when she heard footsteps coming toward her. Maybe it was Zeke returning with Mirac. Or maybe it was someone else. She couldn't take that chance.

Cassie froze for just a moment and then ducked into the closest room, letting the door slide shut behind her. She held her breath and pressed her ear to the door, hoping to hear Zeke. She listened to the footsteps growing louder and louder. Then suddenly they stopped, and Cassie heard a familiar voice. Cardeklpe! It might be all right if the leader of T.O.E. knew about her and Ben. But no—Zeke had said absolutely no one should see her.

Quickly Cassie looked around for a place to hide. She was in one of the sleeping chambers, and the few pieces of furniture were anchored to the floor. Just as she was about to panic, Cassie saw the small closet door at the far end of the room. She lunged for it, sliding into the darkness just as the door to the room opened and Cardeklpe and another Triminican entered.

Opening the closet door a tiny crack, Cassie watched the two aliens. They each sat down on a bed, jabbering away in Triminican. Or at least Cassie thought it was Triminican. She had the odd feeling that they had switched languages at some point. But she brushed the thought from her head. She simply wasn't used to hearing Triminican spoken yet.

After ten minutes crouched in the small closet, Cassie's legs were cramping, and she started to consider revealing herself. What was the worst thing that could happen to her? Immediately, pictures of what the orphan colony must look like sprang into her mind. She decided to stay hidden. It was a wise decision. Because at that moment Cardeklpe rose from where he sat, crossed the room, and locked the door. Then, breathing a sigh of relief, he reached up and removed his face.

CHAPTER

Cardeklpe dropped the face on the floor. Cassie glanced down at the human features now staring up at the ceiling and felt a wave of nausea wash over her. Then slowly she raised her eyes and looked at the alien. Beneath the human mask was a—a—the first word that sprang to Cassie's mind was *owl*. The creature had a round, flat face, with enormous oval eyes suspended over a beak. Except that the beak wasn't small like an owl's. It was long and hooked like a vulture's.

The other alien peeled off his face and threw it on the floor next to Cardeklpe's. Then he scratched at his bird face as if it itched. Cassie felt her knees buckling but steadied herself. It was more important than ever that she stay hidden. These creatures were not Triminicans. But who, or what, were they?

For many long minutes Cassie watched the strange creatures strut around the room and talk. Who could they be? How did they get here? How many of them were there? Cassie's imagination ran a marathon.

At last there was a knock on the door. Cardeklpe dove for the human faces. The two aliens quickly disguised themselves again, and then Cardeklpe opened the door. Cassie breathed a sigh of relief. It was Zeke.

"Mirac wants to see you," he said to Cardeklpe in English.

Cardeklpe nodded and left the room, the other creature following behind him.

"Cassie?" Zeke whispered.

Cassie pushed the closet door open and fell out, her knees locked in the crouching position. Zeke ran to help her.

"Oh, Zeke. I'm so glad to see you! How did you know I was here?"

"Spot and I searched the entire ship. We could not find you. This was the only sleep chamber we could not get inside." Zeke looked around the room. "Spot was right behind me. I wonder what happened to him."

"Zeke, I have so much to tell you," said Cassie. "I'm sorry I left that room, but I was looking for Ben."

Zeke nodded. "As am I. We were hoping he was with you. Mirac is furious."

"Really? He's angry?" Cassie was surprised.

"He is as angry as a Triminican gets!" said Zeke.

"Zeke, listen—those people are not Triminicans!" Cassie exclaimed.

"Who? What do you mean?" asked Zeke, alarmed.

"The ones who were just in this room. They're not human. They're not Triminican. They—they're owls or something."

"Owls? What is an owl?"

"It's a bird. They look like giant birds. They took their faces off and . . ."

Cassie gasped.

Another member of T.O.E. was standing in the doorway. In one of his powerful fists, he clutched Ben O'Brien's hair. Beneath it was Ben with a wild look in his eyes. He was struggling like crazy to get away. But the alien barely flinched.

"Well, well," he snarled in English. "There are two of them, are there?"

"Cassie!" cried Ben.

Zeke jumped in front of Cassie protectively.

"Who are you? What do you want?" he said.

The alien smirked at Zeke.

"The question really is, What are *you* doing in Cardeklpe's chambers? *I* have brought our leader a gift."

"Gift?" shrieked Ben, struggling harder.

The alien laughed. It was a horrible cackle, and it sent chills up and down Cassie's spine.

"I guess now I will have *two* gifts for Cardeklpe. This should make him quite popular when we reach home. And quite rich!"

Abruptly the alien stopped laughing. The color drained from his face, his eyes rolled back in his head, and, letting go of Ben's hair, he hit the floor with a thud. Standing behind him, a strange-looking device in his hand, was Spot.

"Spot!" said Zeke. "There you are!"

"I determined that you would be in need of assistance when I observed—"

Zeke cut the robot off in midsentence.

"There is no time for an explanation right now," he said, springing to the doorway and glancing down the hall.

"Wha—what happened to him?" asked Ben, rubbing his head and looking down at the alien.

"The robot used a stunzapper on him," said Zeke proudly. "Hurry! The effects are only good for a few minutes."

Following Zeke's orders, Cassie and Ben helped drag the body into the room where they had first watched the Earth disappear beneath them. Zeke closed and locked the door. Then he turned and faced his friend.

"Cassie, show me this owl," he demanded.

Cassie bent over the unconscious man and carefully peeled off his face.

"Whoa!" cried Ben. "He looks like . . . like . . ."

"An owl?" said Cassie.

"Yeah. Like an owl. Only he's got a beak like an eagle."

"No way!" said Cassie. "That's a vulture beak!"

Zeke stood frozen while Cassie and Ben argued about birds. When Cassie finally glanced up and saw the horrified expression on her friend's face, she knew that they were in big trouble.

"Did Cardeklpe have this face also?" Zeke asked softly, his eyes never moving from the owlman on the floor.

"Yes," said Cassie breathlessly. "Who are they?"

"They are Delphs," said Zeke. "We must restrain him before he wakes."

"With what?" asked Cassie, looking around the empty room.

"Robot!" ordered Zeke.

Spot produced a roll of rope from a compartment on his side. Together Cassie and Ben bound the Delph's hands and feet. Then Zeke ripped off a section of the alien's shirt and, wincing, stuffed it gently into his mouth.

"Guard him," Zeke instructed Cassie. "No matter what happens, do not let him go. Spot, come with me."

Zeke and Spot left the room. Cassie looked at Ben. He was crouched next to the Delph, his eyes popping out of his head, his tongue hanging out of his mouth.

"Scared now?" Cassie asked the bully.

"Me? Of course not!" Ben barked.

"You should be," said Cassie.

A commotion out in the hall brought them

71

both to the door. Cardeklpe was yelling again. Only this time it was Zeke's voice that responded calmly to each outburst.

A moment later the sound of door after door being opened and slammed shut echoed through the ship. Cassie held her breath and waited. Cardeklpe must be determined to find them. And that meant it was only a matter of time before she and Ben ended up on the orphan colony planet.

Or worse.

The owl-man woke while Cassie and Ben were still listening at the door. Hearing him moan behind them, they both swung around. The alien's huge owl eyes flashed furiously as he began rolling across the floor, trying to loosen the cord around his hands and feet.

"What should we do?" whispered Cassie.

"How should I know?" snapped Ben.

"I don't know how you should know, Ben," Cassie snapped back. "But stop being such a jerk, will you? This *is* all your fault, you know."

Cassie took a deep breath and stepped toward the Delph with her most menacing look.

"STOP!" she commanded. But the Delph completely ignored her.

At that instant the door burst open, sending Ben flying across the room and into the struggling owl-man. With a yelp of fear, Ben jumped away just as Cardeklpe and his friend entered the room. They were still wearing their human masks.

"Well, well, well . . . what have we here?" sneered Cardeklpe.

The Delph on the floor moaned and rolled his eyes.

"Untie him!" Cardeklpe ordered his companion. The alien obeyed and brushed past Ben and Cassie to aid his fellow Delph.

Thundering footsteps brought Zeke, Spot, and Mirac into view. Cassie calmed down as they entered the room behind Cardeklpe.

Mirac took one look at the Delph on the floor and then raised his eyes to meet Cardeklpe's. The two leaders faced each other in silence.

"You have deceived me," Mirac stated.

"And you me," said Cardeklpe. "You said no specimens were to be allowed on board. Yet you have brought two Earth children back with you."

"The Earth children are here by accident," said Mirac. "We will take them to Triminica, where we will provide food and shelter for them until we can return them to their planet."

Cardeklpe chuckled an evil, gravelly laugh.

"Obviously you do not know who I am."

"If you are who I assume you to be, everyone in our galaxy knows you," Mirac responded.

Cardeklpe puffed up proudly.

"Then you know also that we are wanted on Triminica for crimes against the state. We

74

would be executed if we landed there."

"We do not perform executions on Triminica!" Zeke chimed in.

"We send all criminals to the prison planet," said Mirac, "as agreed upon by all civilized beings of the Interplanetary Justice League."

Cardeklpe snorted. "Delphon does not belong to that absurd league of yours."

Mirac changed the subject. "How many of you are there on board my ship?" he demanded.

"What's the matter, Triminican?" growled the Delph. "Afraid you are outnumbered?"

"Arrival at Transport Station 712 in sixteen minutes," droned Spot.

"I have a ship to land!" said Mirac. "I have no time for this conversation. You will leave the Earth children and come with me."

Cardeklpe laughed wildly and ripped his face off, throwing it against a wall of the room and jumping to block Mirac's path. He leaned his owl face in close to the Triminican.

"Look closely at this face!" he growled. "I have been stranded on that backward planet Earth for two years. But I have not forgotten that we are sworn enemies. You, on the other hand, seem to have forgotten that this transport station is under Delph control."

Mirac did not flinch.

"Are you certain?" he said calmly. "You have been gone two years. Much has changed."

Cassie thought she saw a look of uncertainty cross the Delph's face.

"You are bluffing!" he snarled.

"Am I?" said Mirac.

And with that, the Triminican turned and left the room. Everyone followed in his path. Cassie tried to linger behind but found herself being pushed into the crowd by a Delph.

"So this Card . . . Cardek . . . whoever. Who is he?" she whispered to Zeke, who walked by her side.

"His real name is Trill," answered Zeke. "He and his band of criminals escaped while being transported to our prison planet two years ago. No one knew what happened to them. He is a very powerful man on Delphon."

"Are all the members of T.O.E. really Delphs?"

Zeke shrugged his shoulders. "I do not know."

Later, in the control room, Cassie and Ben stood side by side, their eyes glued to Mirac as he piloted the spaceship. They did not talk, not daring to voice their fears. An uneasy silence had come over the ship.

Suddenly Zeke pushed his way between Ben and Cassie and whispered, "Turn around and look!"

Both Earth children obeyed immediately, turning to gaze out the ship's window. They were almost at the transport station now, and signs of civilization were appearing in the sky outside the spaceship. Except that the signs were not flashing neon billboards advertising amid the stars for restaurants and amusement parks, the way Cassie had hoped they would be. They were large arrows of dark twisted wire, pointing only at a dimly lit runway as if to say, Land or crash, we don't care. With a sinking feeling, Cassie suddenly knew the truth.

"The Delphs do have control here, don't they?" she whispered.

Zeke said nothing. But Cassie felt his hand squeeze hers.

"What are we going to do?" Ben whined softly.

"You are going to run!" said Zeke so quietly that Cassie thought she had heard him wrong.

"What?" she whispered.

"As Triminicans, we are protected here," Zeke whispered back. "They can threaten us, even lock us up for a time. But they would not dare hurt us. Our high counsel will learn of our landing and come for us. But as unaccompanied minors, you two can be transported anywhere from the orphan colony to Delphon."

"What would happen to us on Delphon?" asked Cassie.

"You do not want to know."

"So where will we run?" whispered Ben.

"Out of the terminal and into the park."

"What park?" asked Cassie.

"It is called the Argosy Arcadium. But you will not be able to read the lettering, anyway. It is an amusement park left over from the days when a more peaceful people controlled this transport station."

"Does it still work?" asked Ben.

"No," said Zeke. "But we have heard of an underground network there that can help you." He paused, lowering his voice still further. "Enter through the maze."

Mirac called out something in Triminican.

"We are landing," Zeke said in a normal voice. "Follow me."

As Cassie and Ben followed Zeke out of the room, Cardeklpe called after them.

"Do not leave this room."

"The Earth creatures need to gather their belongings," said Zeke. "We will return."

"NO!" said the owl-man.

Suddenly there was a loud crackle of static, and a voice came through a speaker on the control panel. Mirac leaned in to respond, but before he could open his mouth, Trill answered, identifying the ship as under Delph control.

When Mirac struggled to regain command, the room instantly filled with Delphs. A shiver ran up and down Cassie's spine as she counted the number of menacing owl faces in the room. Thirteen. Thirteen Delphs. And with their masks off, they looked scarier than ever. Cassie felt her stomach leap into her throat as she tried to imagine what could be worse than an orphan colony.

Trill permitted Mirac to land the spaceship but kept control of the speaker device. Then he ordered all the real Triminicans on board the ship to line up and file out. As each one reached the top of the staircase, Trill checked them closely, making certain none of them were human. Cassie and Ben were forced to sit in a corner and wait until everyone else had left the ship. As Cassie watched Zeke leave, she had a horrible feeling that her whole life was about to change—for the worse.

When they were finally allowed off the ship, Cassie and Ben were ushered down a long corridor and shoved roughly into a room. Cassie wasn't sure what she expected: A big terminal bustling with excitement? Creatures of every shape and color racing in all directions? A giant passport line? All she knew was that she definitely did not expect to be sitting on the floor of a plain, windowless room the size of the average bathroom on Earth.

Ben looked around the room and groaned.

"We're in prison," he said.

Cassie stood up and examined the room carefully. There were two doors—the one she and Ben had just been shoved through and one across from it on the opposite wall. Neither had doorknobs or any visible way of being opened. There were two chairs and one table. The overhead light was just a bare bulb.

"It isn't a prison, Ben," said Cassie. "It's an interrogation room."

"What do they want to interrogate us about?" whined Ben. "We're just kids."

Cassie ignored him. She wanted to prepare herself for anything that happened. Okay. So someone or something would ask her questions. Then they would send her to the orphan colony. Or to Delphon. Her best chance would be to escape *before* she arrived at either of those horrible places. Run, Zeke had said. Run and we will find you.

The door opened and Trill entered, followed by four Delphs in identical uniforms. Moving away from the cluster of owl faces, Cassie pressed her back against the farthest wall. She crossed her arms and waited, eyes glued to the door that Trill had left open behind him. Ben took a place on the wall a few feet from Cassie.

"Hello, Cassie," Trill sneered.

Cassie froze her face in her meanest look and said nothing.

"I said hello," Trill repeated, louder this time. "You will respond."

Again, Cassie just glared at him.

Swiftly one of the Delphs in uniform moved toward Cassie and grasped her arm in a tight grip, his vulture beak practically touching Cassie's nose.

"The great Trill has spoken to you. Answer him!" he spat into Cassie's face.

Cassie swallowed hard.

"The great Trill?" she said, trying to sound sarcastic but sounding more like a mouse.

"Ahh, she does speak!" snarled one of the other Delphs. He turned his attention toward Ben. "And the male? Does he speak also?"

"Yes, yes—I speak!" said Ben.

Trill laughed. "This particular female is braver than this individual male," he said.

"What?" sputtered Ben, his face turning red. "Are you calling me a coward?"

Eagerly all the Delphs in the room turned toward Ben, hoping for some display of Earth emotion.

It was just the kind of opening that great spies look for. Cassie acted quickly before she lost her chance. Swiftly she stomped her foot as hard as she could on the instep of the Delph holding her. He let go with a yelp of pain, and hollering, "NOW, BEN!" Cassie dove past the Delphs and out the open door.

The hustling, bustling, packed-with-aliens-of-all-races terminal she had expected before now spilled out around Cassie as she ran. But she had no time to enjoy it. She was sure she was being followed. And though she wondered where Ben was, she was not going to turn around. She had to get out of the terminal—and fast!

She ran. She ran until her sides ached and her legs ached and she was gasping for breath. She heard panting beside her and hoped it was Ben.

83

She raced toward the opposite end of the terminal, past the shops with the signs she could not read and the stands selling food whose smells she could not identify. Finally she raced out into the open air and stopped, overwhelmed by the amount of activity outside, the two suns shining down on the planet, and all the creatures milling everywhere. Ben skidded to a stop beside her.

"Don't stop, Cass," he gasped. "They're right behind us."

"I . . . I can't run anymore," gasped Cassie, clutching her side.

"Sure you can! Just turn around and look!"

Cassie peeked over her shoulder and saw the throng of Delphs racing after them. She and Ben looked at each other and, without another word, broke back into a run. But they were moving more slowly now, and the two suns were beating down on them, and every muscle in Cassie's body was aching.

And then suddenly Ben was not beside her anymore.

Cassie panicked. It was true that this was all Ben's fault. And he *was* a total jerk. But at the moment he was the only other human within a million-mile radius, and she really, really wished he hadn't disappeared. She felt tears welling up inside of her. Spies don't cry, she reminded herself. But she was exhausted and scared. Where *was* he?

Frantically she turned as she ran, searching for some sign of Ben. It was a mistake. She tripped over a rock of some sort and found herself lying facedown in the dirt, listening to the thundering footsteps and cries of the Delphs growing louder and louder.

"Cassie, get up!"

Now she was hearing things.

"CASSIE!"

She looked up weakly. It was Ben, driving some sort of flying golf cart. Cassie sprang to her feet and hopped on board. Ben floored the engine.

The vehicle was fast, and Ben was great at maneuvering around the other vehicles and creatures on the roadways outside the main terminal.

Cassie gave herself a moment to calm down, enjoying the breeze that dried the sweat that had broken out all over her body. When she could breathe normally again, she looked over at Ben and grinned.

"I can't believe it! This is probably the smartest thing you've ever done in your whole life!"

"I know!" Ben's face was one giant grin as he drove. "Aren't you impressed?"

"Totally! Where did you learn to drive, anyway? And where did you get this thing?"

"There was a whole bunch of them just sitting at the curb over there," said Ben, taking a hand off the wheel for a second and waving it wildly behind him. "This group of creatures that I guess were drivers or something were standing nearby. I just jumped in and turned the key. Can you believe it? It drives just like a go-cart!"

"Where are we going?" asked Cassie.

"I have no idea."

"Let's look for the amusement park," Cassie suggested.

A siren howled behind them, and Cassie and Ben looked at each other in fear.

"They're still chasing us!" said Cassie.

"What should we do?" asked Ben.

"Hide," said Cassie. "Let's ditch this thing and hide."

"I've got a better idea," said Ben. "Let's do what they do in the movies back home!"

"What do you mean?"

"Let's fake our own death! See that building in the field over there?"

"Yeah."

"I'm going to turn off this road and head straight for it. We'll jump out into the field just before the golf cart crashes into the building."

Cassie was amazed.

"That's great, Ben. Only . . . could you slow down a little before we jump?"

The sirens were louder now.

"Ready?" asked Ben.

"Ready!" said Cassie.

Ben veered off into the field and slowed the

vehicle just a bit. Cassie shut her eyes and held her breath as they headed straight for the building.

"JUMP!" shouted Ben.

Cassie jumped.

A second after she landed with a thud in a clump of bushes, Cassie heard an explosion and opened her eyes. The cart was gone. In its place was a raging fire, which was rapidly spreading to the building.

Something moved at the corner of Cassie's vision, and she watched as Ben rose from where he had landed in the open field and darted to her side. Together they crouched behind the clump of bushes and watched as several vehicles, sirens wailing, pulled up at the fire. Dozens of Delphs climbed out of the golf carts and began combing the area for some sign of the Earthlings. Cassie knew that she and Ben had to move fast. She looked around for someplace to hide. And that was when she saw it looming ahead in the distance. It looked just like the top of a roller coaster on Earth. The amusement park!

CHAPTER

15

"Ben, look! The amusement park!"

In a flash, the two humans were up on their feet and running toward the top of the roller coaster. It was farther away than it looked, and after fifteen minutes Ben and Cassie were once again sweating in the heat of the two suns. But there no longer seemed to be anyone following them, so they slowed their pace and walked for a while.

"Hey, Cass," said Ben.

"Yeah?"

"I guess I'm kind of sorry."

"You *guess* you're *kind of* sorry? Is that an apology?"

"Yeah," grumbled Ben. "I guess," he added.

"What are you apologizing for?" asked Cassie.

"I didn't believe you about the orphan colony. I didn't believe you when you said you weren't going up into outer space. I just thought it would be a lot of fun to ride in a spaceship and get to spy with you and Zeke."

"Why would I lie about that stuff, Ben?"

"Well, what *were* you doing on the spaceship?"

Cassie stopped walking and stared at Ben.

"I was saying good-bye to my best friend. Just like I would if any friend was moving out of town. Wouldn't you?"

Ben squirmed uncomfortably. "I don't know. I guess I don't have very many friends."

"You're a bully, Ben. Bullies never have friends," said Cassie as she started walking again.

Ben caught up with her.

"All I'm saying is that I really didn't mean to get us into this kind of trouble," said Ben. "I mean, I guess this is just about the stupidest thing I ever did."

Cassie smiled. "Yeah, but that golf cart thing was the smartest. So maybe you're a lot smarter than you think."

"Hey!" Ben practically shouted. "I like that!"

Ten minutes later they reached the entrance to the park. But there were no ticket booths, no ticket takers, no people at all. There was only a circular door, with a large red button next to it covered with lettering Cassie could not read.

"This must be the maze," she said to Ben, who shrugged.

Cassie took a deep breath and pressed the button. Immediately the circular door opened. Cassie peered inside. It looked like a maze. Should they risk it? What if they couldn't get out?

No one would ever know where they were. Well, Zeke would. But where was he, anyway?

"Zeke *did* say the underground people were on the other side of this, didn't he?" she asked.

"Yeah," said Ben. "That's what he said."

"Well," said Cassie, leaning forward and squinting into the maze. "Do you think we should enter together or one at a time?"

Suddenly there were footsteps behind them.

"Cassie!" cried Ben.

Cassie whirled around and saw two owl creatures heading straight for them. She turned to say something to Ben. But he was gone. She looked around anxiously and then realized he had entered the maze without her and the door had closed behind him.

Frantically Cassie punched at the red button again. The door opened, and Cassie ran into the maze. She heard the door slam behind her and whirled around to make sure she hadn't been followed inside. But the door was gone. In its place was a corridor: A rounded tunnel with no walls, no windows, no doors. And no Ben.

Cassie turned quickly—and found herself staring down an identical tunnel. She turned again, and another tunnel appeared. No matter which direction she faced, a tunnel appeared, stretching out before her with no end in sight. Cassie reminded herself that the maze was a game. There simply had to be a way out. She closed her eyes and stepped into the nearest tunnel.

But when she opened her eyes, Cassie was dismayed to find four more corridors, narrower and brighter than the ones before. Each time she chose a tunnel, more choices appeared. And each time the tunnels became smaller and brighter. Was this some sicko's idea of a fun house? Cassie called out Ben's name, but it bounced off the walls and echoed back at her.

Half an hour later she was down on her hands and knees, crawling through yet another tunnel, squinting against the bright light, cursing Ben O'Brien in her mind. This was all his fault. Apologies or no apologies, this was still all his fault. And where was he now, anyway? Maybe when she got out of this stupid maze she could strike a bargain with the Delphs. She could sell Ben out, and he would go to the orphan colony while she returned to Earth.

If she ever got out, she reminded herself as the next set of tunnels forced her onto her stomach. As she slithered along, Cassie plotted her revenge. Then she remembered that Ben had saved her life back at the terminal, and she felt guilty. Then she thought about his apology and felt guiltier still. Where was he, anyway? Where was Zeke? And where was the end of this maze and the underground network Zeke had talked about?

Suddenly Cassie found herself plunging downward into blackness. Faster and faster she fell, like Alice through the rabbit hole. And then just as suddenly she stopped falling. She was lying on a sea of foam. And she was outside. She was out of the maze! She was free!

"Well, well, look what we have here!" said a voice directly above Cassie. She looked up—into the huge owl eyes of a Delph.

"Get up, Earthling!"

Cassie swallowed the lump in her throat. Maybe if she pretended to be dead they would take her to a hospital and . . .

"I said GET UP!" The Delph kicked at Cassie's leg. Cassie sprang to her feet and started running toward the roller coaster. But she was already exhausted, and the searing heat burned her lungs each time she gasped for air. The Delph was so close she could feel his breath on the back of her neck. This was it. She was doomed. She would spend the rest of her life on a planet of . . .

And then she saw it.

It was a small opening in a fence surrounding an abandoned ride. Small enough for a human child to squeeze through. But too small for an adult Delph.

With a burst of energy, Cassie leaped for the hole and squeezed herself through—and immediately discovered that the only thing on the other side was a wall. She was trapped in a hole like an animal. And a Delph arm was reaching in to grab her.

"Leave me alone!" Cassie screamed, hitting the arm. If only she could stall for time, maybe the underground would suddenly spring to her aid.

But the arm was persistent. It grabbed hold of her leg.

Cassie bit the arm.

It withdrew with a yelp.

Then suddenly another arm darted quickly in and out, and Cassie felt a stinging in her leg. Everything began to turn upside down, and then her world was filled with darkness.

CHAPTER 16

When Cassie woke up, the first thing she saw was Ben's face peering down at her.

"Great! You're up! It's about time!" he said, entirely too cheerfully.

Cassie groaned and held her head.

"Why are you so cheerful?" she muttered.

"I'm pretending I'm not scared," whispered Ben.

"Why?"

Ben shrugged. "I don't know. It seemed like a good idea. I was worried about you, Cass. You've been out for a long time."

Cassie groaned again and sat up.

"What happened? Where are we?"

Ben sat down next to her and handed her a glass of liquid.

"Drink this. It will make you feel better."

Cassie looked fuzzily at the glass in his hand.

"Where'd it come from?"

"From them!" said Ben. "It's okay. I've already

had some. It really does make you feel better."

Cassie stared at the glass suspiciously.

"I swear it's okay, Cass. There's food, too. They're fattening us up for the kill or something."

"Very funny," said Cassie, though she knew he wasn't kidding. She took the glass and sipped the liquid. It tasted cool and refreshing and slightly salty. She drained the glass and felt much better.

"So, where are we?" she repeated her question.

"In prison," Ben said simply. "They're keeping us here for a while and then taking us someplace else. That's all I could figure out. By the way— stay on your bed."

"Why?"

"Take a good look. This place is made of glass or plastic or something, and all the walls are curved. It's really hard to move around."

Cassie looked and realized that not only was Ben right, but they were in one of maybe a dozen similar bubbles, all floating in space.

"Have you tried to find a way out?"

"I tried to throw myself against the glass. But I couldn't get enough of a running start." Ben rubbed his arm at the memory. "Besides, even if we broke out, it's a really long fall to the ground."

Cassie sighed. "We've just got to find a way out before they send us to the orphan colony."

"Cassie, I don't know how to tell you this. But

I think these creeps are going to sell us to someone for some kind of experiments."

"We're not going to the orphan colony?"

"Actually, you're both correct!" said a voice as Trill floated into view. He was in the passenger seat of a small vehicle driven by one of the owl creatures. Another Delph stood on a small platform attached to the back fender. They seemed to be driving on air.

The vehicle stopped right beneath Ben and Cassie's bubble. Trill reached up and opened a small hatch at the bottom.

"We are going to *lend* you to a scientific community," he called up. "After they've finished experimenting on you, you'll go to the orphan colony. So you see, you're both right!" He cackled wildly. Cassie thought she was going to be sick.

"Here we go!" he called with another evil chortle.

Neither Cassie nor Ben moved.

"Out!" Trill ordered.

Cassie and Ben glanced at each other and by silent agreement remained motionless.

"If I have to come up and get you, I promise it will be painful," Trill threatened.

That was enough. Cassie and Ben both jumped toward the bottom of the bubble, arriving at the exit at the same time. Once outside, they settled into the seats Trill pointed at, and the vehicle moved slowly through a field of bubbles, out into a domed room, and finally out of the building and into the open air.

Cassie racked her brain for a way to escape. She could think of nothing except maybe trying to knock the Delph at the back of the vehicle off the platform. But she and Ben had nowhere to go. For the first time in her short spying career, Super Sleuth Cassie Williams was completely without ideas.

So she settled into her seat and did what she thought all spies did in these situations: kept her eyes open for an opportunity to escape.

Fifteen minutes later the vehicle landed in front of a building with huge black letters on the outside. Cassie didn't need to understand the writing to know that this was a place to be feared. The vehicle stopped next to what looked like a giant letter slot in a mailbox. The owl creature in back hopped off the platform, plucked Ben from his seat, and threw him into the mail slot. When he reached for Cassie, she screamed and struggled, but to no avail. The next thing she knew, she had plunged through the mail slot and landed on top of Ben.

"Where are we?" asked Ben as they scrambled to their feet.

Cassie looked around at the antiseptic room and broke out in a cold sweat.

"What does it look like, Ben?" she snapped.

"A hospital," said Ben.

"And here come the doctors," Cassie said, her voice shaking.

Three creatures approached them, one large and two small, all clothed in floor-length hooded robes. Their faces were covered in dark plastic shields.

"I guess they think we're contagious," said Cassie.

"I hope we are," said Ben. He blew air at the small creature closest to him, but it did not even fog up the shield.

The larger creature silently motioned for them to move, and Cassie and Ben found themselves being followed down a dark corridor, pushed out another mail slot and then into another waiting vehicle. The large creature leaped into the driver's seat while the two smaller ones climbed on back with Cassie and Ben.

"Now where are we going?" moaned Ben.

Slowly one of the small creatures removed its shield, revealing a familiar face.

"Home," said Zeke. "You are going home."

CHAPTER 17

"Zeke!" cried Cassie, throwing her arms around her friend.

"Not now, Cassie," said Zeke as another transport vehicle whizzed past them. "We are not out of danger yet."

"But how did you find us? Where are we going? Who's driving—Mirac?" Cassie let all the questions tumble out at once.

"There will be plenty of time for that later," said Zeke, grinning. "Spot, any sign of a chase?"

"Negative," reported the other small robed creature.

The driver made a sharp right, increased the speed of the vehicle, and drove expertly around a building and out into open space.

Cassie had just breathed a sigh of relief when she heard the siren. She turned in her seat and saw with a jolt that no less than five small vehicles were chasing them.

"Chase has been given," reported Spot.

"Increase speed!" ordered Zeke, his eyes glued to the vehicles in pursuit.

Cassie and Ben were thrown back in their seats by the sudden increase in speed of the tiny vehicle. But the fleet of five were still gaining on them. Suddenly one of the vehicles burst out of the pack and advanced. Within seconds it was so close that Cassie could see what looked like a weapon being aimed directly at them by an enormous owl creature.

"They will be within firing range in one point three seconds," Spot reported.

"You know what to do," said Zeke.

Something inside the robot whizzed. Then something whirred. And suddenly his arm shot out, and a long, thick wire with a bulging magnet at the end burst out of his hand socket. The magnet sped through space, drawing the wire out behind it. With a snap it attached itself to the front of the pursuing vehicle. At the exact moment the owl creature fired, Spot yanked on the wire, spinning the Delphs' small ship off course.

To the horror of the firing Delph, the bullets scattered across the sky behind him, not at the fleeing Triminicans but at the other four vehicles in the Delph fleet. One by one, the four tiny ships fell away, trying desperately to dodge the shots.

"Robot detach!" Zeke ordered.

The robot retrieved the magnet.

"Activate the thrusters," Zeke commanded the driver.

As they raced off into the sky, Cassie grabbed on to her seat for safety. But her eyes were glued to the point in the sky where there had once been five Delph vehicles. Now there was one.

They traveled through open space for what seemed like hours. Zeke and Spot kept watch, constantly consulting on the identity of small passing vehicles and talking in a mixture of Triminican and English. Cassie and Ben gazed in wonder at the stars and planets. Cassie had a million questions she wanted to ask her alien friend. But she knew better than to bother him right now.

Finally the tiny ship slowed and began to circle a moon. As they reached its dark side, Cassie saw that a spaceship lay waiting for them. It was enormous—much larger than the one that had first landed the Triminicans on Earth.

Ben and Cassie watched in awe as two panels on the side of the ship separated and the small ship they were riding in was driven right inside the larger one. Once inside, Zeke sprang from his seat and raced off with Spot, leaving Cassie and Ben alone with the driver, who made sure the smaller ship was secure and then silently motioned for Ben and Cassie to follow.

As they walked the corridors of the large vessel, Cassie could feel the engines revving up and the ship moving out of dock. She wondered where they were going.

As they entered the main room, Mirac looked up from the control panel and smiled.

"Welcome!" he said. "Please stay out of the way."

Cassie turned to look at the driver of the small vehicle in amazement. She had just assumed that *it* was Mirac.

The driver removed the visor.

"Inora!" cried Cassie.

"Cassie," said Inora, smiling. She placed her visor in a small bin anchored to the floor and took up a position at one of the windows. Cassie saw that Zeke was on watch out a different window. Spot manned a section of the control panel.

"Cassie, sit," said Zeke.

Cassie obediently found a seat near a window and motioned for Ben to do the same. For a while they traveled alone in the open sky. But as they neared Transport Station 712, a fleet of Delph ships moved out silently to greet them.

"Zekephlon!" commanded Mirac.

"I am ready," Zeke responded.

Cassie glanced at Zeke and saw him focused on the ships out one of the windows, a remote control unit in his hand.

"Wait until they are close enough," said Mirac.

"One of the Delph ships arming to fire!" reported Spot.

"And, six, five, four . . . ," Zeke counted down, his hand poised above a button on the remote.

"Delph ship firing!" said Spot.

"NOW, ZEKEPHLON!" Mirac ordered.

Zeke punched a button on the remote unit at the exact moment that Cassie felt the impact of the hit. She slid to the floor as Mirac lost control of the ship for a moment. Then she curled into a ball and waited for the next hit.

But it never came. Mirac steadied the ship.

"Well done, Zekephlon!" he said to his son. "Robot—damage report."

"Minimal damage," reported Spot. "Repairs can be rendered in transit."

Cassie was stunned. She scrambled to her feet and looked out the window. The sky was purple and filled with stars. She could not see the Delph ships anywhere.

"Did you destroy that entire fleet of ships?" she asked, amazed.

"No," said Zeke. "But we fired an unusually large tranquilizer canister at them. One of our Triminican scientists supplied us with it. The Delphs will float in space until they wake up."

"When will that be?" asked Ben from his position on the floor.

Zeke shrugged.

"It depends on how much gas they took in. I suppose an entire crew could wake a week from now in another galaxy."

"Just as long as it isn't the galaxy we're from!" said Cassie.

"That reminds me," said Mirac. "Next stop, Earth!"

The spaceship soared away from Transport Station 712 and into the deep space that bridged the two galaxies. When the ship was on course, Mirac turned from the control panel and announced that it was time to talk.

"Robot, remain here and alert me to any problems," he said. "Everyone else, follow me."

Mirac, Zeke, Inora, Cassie, and Ben all headed for the spaceship's main room and settled themselves on the cushiony clouds of light that served as chairs. As usual, Cassie started talking immediately.

"So what happened, Zeke? How did you find us? How did you know where we were?"

Zeke laughed. "At first we had no idea," he said. "But when you entered the theme park through the maze the way I told you to, the underground alerted us."

"What?" said Cassie. "They weren't there. We were captured by the Delphs."

"They were there," Zeke explained. "They were just unable to get to you in time. They followed you once you were captured. They spied on the Delphs, and they alerted us to your whereabouts and Trill's plans for you."

"We would not have been able to save you if you had not gone through the maze," said Inora.

"What happened to you while we were running away and being captured?" asked Cassie.

"Mirac is an important man on Triminica!" Zeke announced proudly. "Word of his return had gotten out even as word of Trill's had."

"The high counsel of Triminica had already arranged for our release and that of all the Triminicans traveling with us," Mirac explained.

"You went back to Triminica?" Cassie exclaimed.

Zeke nodded. "But only to arrange for a ship to return you to Earth."

"Wait a minute!" shouted Ben. "You were safely back on your planet, and you risked everything just to help us return to Earth?"

"We did it for Cassie," Zeke explained.

"Yeah, but you saved me, too," said Ben, deep in thought.

"We will return you to your planet," Mirac explained. "We will also search for the Triminicans who are stranded on Earth."

"So Trill didn't lie about that?" asked Cassie.

"A Triminican vessel really did crash on Earth

two years ago," said Mirac. "Trill and his group were aboard that ship. They knew if they were ever going to return to Delphon, they would have to blend in with the Triminicans."

"Wow!" gasped Cassie. "I guess we're lucky the Delphs didn't try to take over Earth."

"I am sure only their fear of what would happen if it were discovered they were aliens stopped them from attempting that," said Mirac.

"So where will you look for these Triminicans?" asked Cassie.

"They are spread all over your planet," said Mirac. "Those who managed to make it back with us have been most helpful. We have a list of all who were aboard the ship and are still unaccounted for. We even think we may know where some of them are."

"And we think another ship of ours might have crashed on Earth about ten months ago," Zeke added. "Mirac and Inora will search for those Triminicans, too."

"Then," said Inora, "in about six months, when the planets are aligned correctly again, we will return home."

"I can't believe you risked everything to help us get home!" Ben repeated.

"Does this mean you will keep our identity a secret?" asked Mirac.

"What? Oh, sure," said Ben, his mind a million miles away.

Zeke and Mirac exchanged a look. Cassie jumped into the conversation.

"Ben would never do anything to put you in danger, would you, Ben?"

"No. I wouldn't!" exclaimed Ben, looking insulted.

"Don't you have something else to say to Zeke and his parents?" Cassie prompted.

"Oh . . . yeah," said Ben sheepishly. "I'm sorry I caused so much trouble."

"Really?" said Zeke, surprised.

"Yeah, really," said Ben. When he saw the suspicious looks on the faces of all the Triminicans, Ben went on.

"I really *am* sorry. Cassie and I were in a lot of danger there, and I should have listened to you when you told me to get off the ship. And I really do promise not to tell anyone who you are. Only . . . can't I tell *anyone* that I rode on a spaceship to outer space?"

A groan rose up from Cassie and the Triminicans.

"Okay, okay," said Ben, laughing. "But can I at least spy with you and Cassie?" he asked Zeke.

"That is up to Cassie," said Zeke.

Ben looked at Cassie.

"I'll think about it," she said, grinning.

"We will rest now," said Mirac, standing up. "The landing on Earth is only two hours away."

*   *   *

Spot woke everyone when Earth came into view. As they took their positions for touchdown, Cassie studied Ben, wondering if he really had changed as much as it seemed or if he was simply too used to being a bully back on Earth.

But as the ship landed, Cassie looked over at Zeke and sighed contentedly. Her best friend was back in town, and that was all that mattered. Cassie and the Spy from Outer Space were an un-beatable team once again.

About the Author

Debra Hess has done a fair amount of spying in her life, and is pretty sure that a few of her friends are from outer space. The author of several popular books for young readers, she lives in Brooklyn, New York, with her husband, a lot of fish, and two newts.